$2.00

This CREEPY,
CRAWLY
book belongs to:

_____

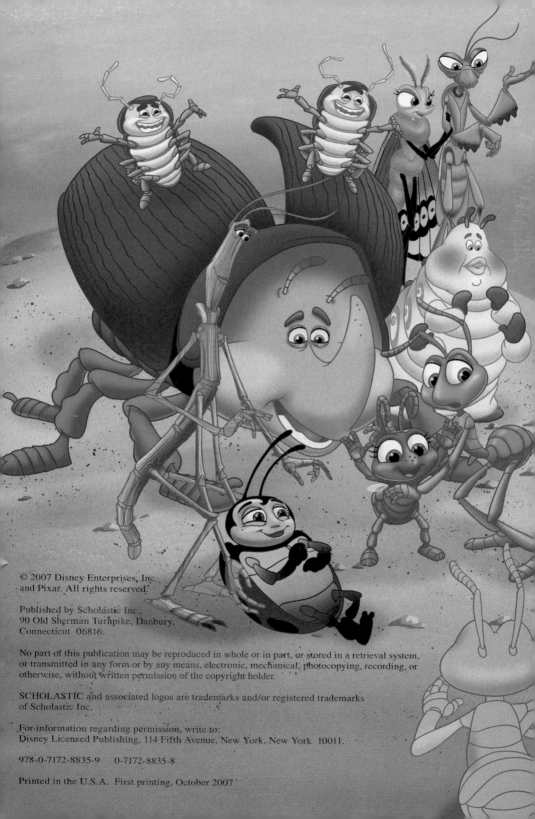

Published by Scholastic Inc.,
90 Old Sherman Turnpike, Danbury,
Connecticut 06816.

For information regarding permission, write to:
Disney Licensed Publishing, 114 Fifth Avenue, New York, New York 10011.

978-0-7172-8835-9   0-7172-8835-8

Printed in the U.S.A. First printing, October 2007

SCHOLASTIC INC.

New York   Toronto   London   Auckland   Sydney
Mexico City   New Delhi   Hong Kong   Buenos Aires

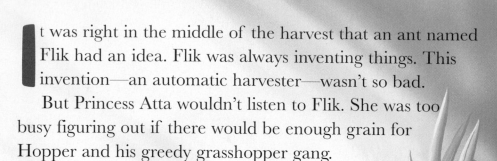

I t was right in the middle of the harvest that an ant named Flik had an idea. Flik was always inventing things. This invention—an automatic harvester—wasn't so bad.

But Princess Atta wouldn't listen to Flik. She was too busy figuring out if there would be enough grain for Hopper and his greedy grasshopper gang.

Every year, the grasshoppers came to demand food from the ants. This year, for the first time, Atta was in charge of the harvest.

Suddenly the ants could hear the grasshoppers coming. Atta was flustered.

The Queen took over. "Food to the offering stone and into the anthill," she said.

The ants left the grasshoppers' grain piled up on the offering stone.

Flik ran for cover, too. But as he was taking off his terrific harvesting machine, he knocked over the offering stone. All the grain slid down into the dry, cracked riverbed.

Hopper, the grasshoppers' leader, was going to be furious.

Hopper was indeed furious. Flik tried to stand up to him but couldn't.

Hopper grabbed Dot, the Queen's youngest daughter, and threatened the terrified ants. "Let's double the order of food. We'll be back at the end of the season!" he snarled.

Flik knew that if the ants obeyed
Hopper, they wouldn't have enough food
for themselves. So he got another idea.
"We could find bigger bugs to come here
and fight," he suggested.

Princess Atta and the Queen
didn't like the idea. But they
were glad to send Flik away.
Only Dot had faith in him.
"Good luck, Flik!" she called as
he floated away on his quest.

Far away from Ant Island, an audience of rowdy
flies was booing yet another circus performance.

P.T. Flea, the circus owner, had enough.
"You're all fired!" he yelled at his performers.

Soon Flik arrived in The City. He had never seen anything like it. This was the place to find tough bugs!

Flik found the out-of-work circus bugs in a run-down tavern. He mistakenly thought they were warriors.

They thought he was looking for circus bugs.

The circus bugs thought Flik was offering them a contract to perform for the ants. So away they flew to Ant Island, dreaming of applause and full-time jobs.

When they got to Ant Island, the circus bugs found out
what the ants expected of them.

Then Rosie the spider told Flik that they were actually
circus bugs.

The circus bugs quietly slipped away.
Flik ran after them, begging them to stay.
Manny the praying mantis spoke for
them all. He said Flik had tricked the bugs
into thinking they'd be in the show.

Flik was about to plead some more when he saw something that terrified him. It was a bird! A bird who ate bugs!

"Run!" he yelled.

As they ran, Flik and the circus bugs saw Dot floating toward them. The bird had spotted Dot, too!

Swiftly, Francis flew up and grabbed the Princess.

While Slim held up Heimlich to distract the bird, Flik and the others helped Dot and Francis escape. Then they all flew into a prickly bush. The bird flew away.

Flik, Dot, and the bugs climbed down from the bush to find the whole ant colony cheering them. What a wonderful sound! The circus bugs had never heard applause before. Right then, the circus bugs decided to help the ants—if Flik could come up with a plan.

Flik did, indeed, have a plan. But he knew that the ants wouldn't listen to him. The plan had to come from the circus "warriors."

Manny was elected to explain the plan to Princess Atta. He told her they would chase the grasshoppers away with a fake bird.

Atta agreed.

The ants stopped collecting grain and helped the bugs build the bird. They liked the idea of little ants defeating big grasshoppers. They also still thought the "warriors" were heroes.

Once the bird was finished, the bugs raised it up into a knothole in the tree. When the time came, Flik would fly it out and give Hopper the scare of his nasty life.

Far away from Ant Island, some of Hopper's gangsters were muttering to one another. Why should they go back to Ant Island? They already had plenty of food.

Hopper didn't agree. "There was that ant that stood up to me," he reminded the gang. "You let one ant stand up to us, they might all stand up," he said adding, "There goes our way of life."

Hopper looked around. Not one grasshopper in his gang dared to disagree with him.

"Let's ride!" he ordered them. With a loud buzz, the gang took off for Ant Island.

Meanwhile, Flik was telling the circus bugs that their work was finished. Because the bird was ready, they wouldn't have to stay and fight.

But now, the circus bugs didn't want to leave. They liked the idea of being heroes.

Then P.T. Flea showed up.
"I'm looking for a bunch of circus
performers," he told the ants.
   Flik tried to hide the truth, but the
ants discovered that their "warrior"
bugs were only circus bugs.

The Queen ordered the circus bugs to leave, and to take Flik with them.

Dot wanted to go with her friends, but her mother held her back.

The ants knew they couldn't fight the grasshoppers alone. Frantically, they started collecting grain again. But there wasn't enough time.

The alarm sounded. The grasshoppers had arrived!

"Mother!" Atta cried. "What do we do?"

The Queen had no answer.

33

The grasshoppers marched on the ants. Hopper had no mercy. He and his gangsters turned the ants into slaves. They were even planning to squish the Queen!

When Dot overheard this, she knew she had to do something. So she sneaked away to find Flik. He would know what to do.

Once Dot convinced Flik to come back, he was ready to fight. She knew his bird idea would work.

The circus bugs wanted to help, too. But they knew P.T. Flea would object, so they shut him up in the wagon.

Then the whole group hurried back to Ant Island.

While the circus bugs were distracting Hopper and his gang with a circus performance, Flik and Dot rallied the ant children. Together, they sneaked up to get the bird ready.

When Gypsy the moth gave the signal, Flik's fake bird zoomed down from the tree, straight at the awful grasshoppers.

Frightened, Hopper and his gang ran!

Then P.T. Flea, who had never understood Flik's plan, escaped. Thinking that the bird was a danger to them all, P. T. Flea set it on fire!

Suddenly Hopper realized that he had been tricked. He quickly got his gang back together.

Once more, the terrible grasshoppers threatened the poor ants. This time, Hopper's target was Atta.

Flik couldn't stand it. "Leave her alone!" he cried.

Flik's action gave the other ants the courage they needed. The rest of the ants and circus bugs joined forces and they attacked.

Hopper knew he couldn't survive if he fought against so many ants. But at least he could get Flik.

Suddenly it started to rain, and everyone ran for cover. During the confusion, Atta was able to grab Flik away from Hopper.

But Hopper wouldn't give up. He chased Flik and Atta across the river.

Flik got another idea. He remembered where the real
bird had its nest. He told Atta where to fly.

When Hopper saw the bird, he laughed. "Another one
of your little bird tricks?" he teased.

But it wasn't.

Bye-bye, Hopper!

The grasshoppers never returned, and the ants never had to worry about food again. The following spring, P.T. Flea's circus set out on a victory tour. A few of the ants wanted to see the world, as Flik had done, and they went along on the tour.

They left Flik with Atta and the rest of the colony. He would be happy inventing things to make ant life easier. He'd had enough of adventure, and home was where he wanted to stay.

EYE SPY

Go on an adventure. Crawl back in the story and find these wild pictures.